The Map

HAMSTERLAND
SQUIRREL PLACE
GERBIL TERRITORY
GERBIL HQ
MOUSELAND
PALACE
TRAINING CAMP FOR MUSKETEERS
MOAT
BELL
KEEP
RIVER
MALONE MANSION AND DUNGEONS
CAMP WHERE TWINS WERE RESCUED.
RATLAND

Chapter 1 - An Adventure

To a land far away,
A mouse went for the day,
To see what it was like.
He discovered no flowers,
No grass or rain showers,
In fact nothing to brighten his hike.

Instead it was dark,
The landscape was stark,
And he shuddered with fear at the thought.
This land was forbidden
All maps of it hidden,
So mice would not go and be caught.

This was the home
Of King Rat, Malone.
What was he thinking to come here?
He was young and hot-headed
His nerves were now shredded,
This son of a Mouse Musketeer.

His dad would be cross,
And concerned for his loss,
Should he fail to return to Mouseland.
At that moment in time,
He was grabbed from behind,
Beaten, gagged and bound foot and hand.

The thugs wanted to know
About his King's come and go,
But the mouse refused all information.
So they beat him some more
While he writhed on the floor
In great pain, while the rats planned invasion.

He awoke all alone,
And wished he was home.
He couldn't move, and he wanted to cry.
His bones were all broken
Couldn't breathe and was choking,
He thought *'this is no way to die.'*

Then the sound of a purr,
And the touch of soft fur
Came from a black and white cat.
"How do you do,
I'm a prisoner here, too
And I want to do something about that"

"I've a plan to escape
But I need you to take
A big part in the proceedings.
When a guard comes this way
Just yell out and say
That your arms and legs are still bleeding."

"When he opens the cell
I'll join in as well,
And offer a peanut butter cake.
They so love the taste
It won't go to waste,
And we'll leave while he's taking his break."

"There is one other thing,"
Said the mouse in some pain,
"I can't walk and my body is reeling."
"Don't worry about that
Just ride on my back,
We are now buddies, together we are leaving."

So all went to plan.
The cat offered the flan,
But the rat was still having some doubt.
If he ate here and now
He'd be as fat as a cow
And the cat and the mouse could get out.

He held open the door
And examined the floor
And the food that was there within reach.
The cat moved an inch,
And it made the rat flinch,
Draw his knife intending to stab each.

With the mouse on his back
The cat started to track
Towards the door where the rat barred his way.
As quick as a flash
Cat with cake made a dash
Towards the exit without delay.

Chapter 1 - An Adventure

Holding on for dear life
Mouse dodged the rat's knife
And hit Rat in the face with the cake.
The brave mouse held on
And the two of them were gone,
Leaving Rat to ponder his mistake.

The cat bounded away
Over filth and decay.
Didn't stop until they reached the border.
The Palace came into view
And safety they knew
Must be the Kingdom's first order.

While still in great pain
The mouse had to explain
To King Mouse what Malone had in store,
For invading the land
And the bad things he planned.
A more menacing threat than before.

Mouse said he was sorry
King said not to worry
His courage he warmly greeted.
He was very concerned
At what he'd just learned.
More important, mouse needed to be treated.

Chapter 1 - An Adventure

A hospital ward
Was where Mouse would record
The place Cat took him off to recover.
He was in so much pain
And would not walk again,
As all were very soon to discover.

Of Mouse they were sad.
But so proud was his dad,
When the King made a fantastic gesture
To rename him Prime
The first parry in escrime.
And the Cat would be called Balestra.

The King then explained
That he wanted trained
Brave injured mice in a new career
Of which Prime would be first
And others would thirst
To be a Wheelchair Musketeer.

The moral of this tale
To keep out of jail
Always listen to your mum and dad.
They know what is best,
It's you needs the test
Of what's right and wrong, good and bad.

Chapter 2 - Triple Trouble - Splash

Three little mice went out to play
In all the wrong places every day.
They diced with death at every turn,
But still they didn't seem to learn.
They took such risks with little fear,
Then one day, BANG! How they paid dear.

First little mouse, Jon, had the bad luck
To run into the road and be squashed by a truck.
The second mouse, Hugh played in water and found
A strong current and weeds and he nearly drowned.
Third mouse, Lee climbed a tree, just to check,
Could he touch the sky? No. Fell down. Broke his neck.

So each was injured and couldn't walk,
Instead they decided to teach and talk
To others so they could be spared
From all the pain and upset they shared.
Their lives were tough but they made do.
They were fit, they fenced, were honest and true.

Chapter 2 - Triple Trouble - Splash

One day while training very late,
Through the gloom saw rats by the Palace gate.
They must have come around the Keep
And passed the guards while the town was asleep.
Oh how the rats laughed they had found a boat
And that's how they managed to cross the moat.

Jon, Hugh and Lee knew they had to warn
All other mice before the dawn.
By then they knew it would be too late
The rats would soon decide their fate.
But when they went to ring the town's bell
They found the rats had stopped that as well.

For they had chewed right through the rope,
Leaving the mice with little hope.
They had to save their Queen and King,
Their homes and friends and everything.
They looked but found the guards were gone.
They'd have to fight the rats alone.

They sat and thought about a plan.
"We need to act as soon as we can,
Can they be tricked or fooled?" said Jon,
"Let's get their leader and then be done.
We have the benefit of complete surprise,
But we'll need to hold them until sunrise."

Chapter 2 - Triple Trouble - Splash

They drew their swords and charged at will.
Chasing the rats back down the hill.
Towards the moat from where they'd come.
Though large in number the rats did run,
Until they had the water in sight
And at that point they turned to fight.

The mice charged on their fear all gone.
Their wheelchairs in the moonlight shone.
With gathering speed they approached their foe.
Leaving the rats nowhere to go.
At water's edge very large in size,
Stood King Rat, Malone – here was their prize.

Fearless Jon fenced quite a few,
But nearer Malone was little mouse, Hugh.
Who used his sword and in one cut-through
Sliced King Rat's trousers and his underpants too.
Then at Malone, Hugh suddenly lunged -
Unable to run, in the moat Malone plunged.

He thrashed about because he couldn't swim,
Fearing the worst Hugh jumped in after him.
King Rat was going down for the third time,
So from the bank Lee threw a lifeline.
Hugh tied it around Malone's ample waist,
Then Jon, Hugh and Lee with Rat to the bank raced.

They managed to haul him out on the side.
They pumped his chest, not sure if he'd died.
He coughed and spluttered was angry and red.
For he realised that all his colleagues had fled.
Although he was bad they knew Rat must live.
Jon, Hugh and Lee needed him as their captive.

The other rats had escaped by boat.
They checked to see that their King would float,
But didn't help him across the moat.
In any case once at the bank
Their leaky vessel promptly sank
And that was the end of their sorry prank.

Far in the distance they heard a cock crow.
Dawn was approaching and the King must know
What had arisen during the night;
How Rats had attacked but had taken flight.
Six o'clock marked changing the guard.
The night staff were found bound and beaten rather hard.

The King was angry when he heard
What night's activities had occurred,
How Malone and his followers attacked Mouseland,
Now he was dishevelled and soaking found.
The King was astounded Malone's demise
Was brought about by three lame mice.

The King addressed Rat with all good grace,
"I fear with your people you've now lost face.
Your threatening behaviour I'll not forget,
For your trouble you've finished bedraggled and wet."
Malone was sent from whence he came.
Told never to attack Mouseland again.

Chapter 2 - Triple Trouble - Splash

When Malone had gone the King spoke to Hugh,
"Although Malone was your foe
You realised he couldn't swim,
And risked your life to rescue him.
You have great courage and love a pond,
I'm going to re-name you Seconde."

The King now spoke to young mouse Jon,
"I'm very proud of what you've done.
I understand you made the plan
To serve your King and save Mouseland,
And in the battle you were fierce
So you will take the new name Tierce."

King finally spoke to young mouse Lee,
"You broke your neck falling from a tree
But here you were doing your best
To save your country from this pest.
Your team is loyal and touches my heart
I think you will suit your new name- Quarte."

"The three of you are very brave
Despite disabilities you gave
Your very best to save this land
From others who were underhand.
Your swordsmanship is superb I hear,
Welcome Wheelchair Musketeers."

My message to you all this day
Is play it safe in every way.
When you want to unwind
A local leisure centre find.
Where you can learn to climb and swim
And have great fun with everything.

If you need to cross the road
Always use the Highway Code.
The Wheelchair Musketeers are brave
But lots of anguish you can save
By playing to your heart's content
In a safe environment.

Chapter 3 - Friendship And Courage

A smart mouse called Ben was just starting school.
Crippled and blind, he was known as a fool,
He was keen and excited and eager to learn,
But fell prey to others who teased him all term.
They thought it was fun to pinch, prod and poke.
He couldn't run away and escape from their joke.

In the same class was the King's youngest son,
Who returned home each evening and relayed what they'd done.
Then one day to school a new student mouse came.
Big Gerald looked tough, but was also lame.
Some spied a new victim, but didn't have the sense
To see this one's physique and he knew how to fence.

The next day Big Gerald was horrified to see
Poor little Ben being tied to a tree.
He realised the bullies were about to inflict
Some nasty surprise on the mouse they had tricked.
Gerald was certainly not going to stand by
While the bullies teased their victim to make him cry.

He drew out his sword and made his demand,
That they release their captive on his command.
The bullies obeyed and let little Ben go.
“We’ll get you another day, Gerald don’t you know.”
Ben thanked him and said, *“I don’t feel of worth,
For I have been crippled like this since birth.”*

Chapter 3 - Friendship And Courage

Gerald *"What's happening here is not very nice.*
I think I could teach you to fence in a trice."
Ben said, "I am so grateful for your concern,
But I cannot see so how will I learn?"
Gerald *"That's quite all right I'll work out a way."*
And little Ben hugged him for brightening his day.

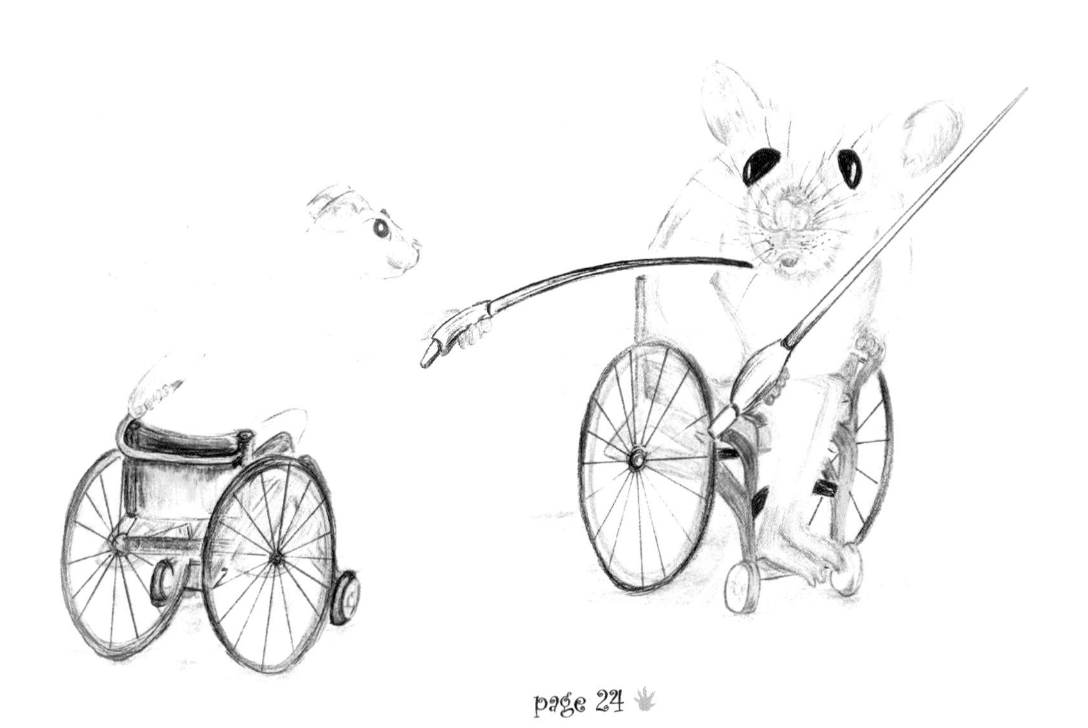

So Gerald and Ben became close like two brothers.
They were really good friends and looked out for each other.
As well as their friendship they realised they knew
The benefits of good food and exercise too.
To stay strong, fit and healthy they ate all their greens,
There was nothing they loved more than vitamins and proteins.

The bullies were mad. This had ruined their plan.
It required a new scheme which they made and began.
They wanted to attack and beat the two mice.
For the humiliation they caused they would now pay the price.
The bullies were slow and ate all the wrong food.
Their manners were bad and they were so rude.

The two friends worked hard as they started to fence.
First little Ben lunged then learned some defence.
Gerald *"Feel the technique and don't be alarmed.*
As long as we are close you won't be harmed.
I'll shout the instructions, as long as you can hear,
Just do I say, you'll have nothing to fear."

Chapter 3 - Friendship And Courage

Ben grew in confidence and took great pride
When given a sword which he wore at his side
And off to school he went with such glee
Big Gerald was his eyes so now he could see.
But after school a tragedy struck
When the bullies attacked and they ran out of luck.

Big Gerald was held and punched to the ground.
Two bullies sat on him and he felt their fists pound.
Little Ben was grabbed and pinned by the throat.
The bullies in full cry oh how they did gloat.
They thought they had won when they force-fed him a bun.
Little Ben choked while the bullies had fun.

Big Gerald was livid, determined and strong.
If they thought this was over the bullies were wrong.
He fought the two brutes so that he could now see
What they were doing to the friend he must free.
Little Ben also fought long and hard
And managed to wriggle free his fencing sword arm.

"Lunge! Lunge!" Big Gerald roared.
So Ben drew his weapon and lunged with his sword
And stabbed a fat bottom that was rather broad.
Bully gave a yelp. Said Ben, *"I think I need some help."*
Gerald *"Oh no you don't, the cowardly bullies have all run away.*
Your timely lunge has saved the day."

Chapter 3 - Friendship And Courage

The whole thing was witnessed by the King's son,
Who again told his father what they had done.
The King was impressed by Gerald and Ben.
And commanded their presence at the palace just then.
Gerald and Ben were now in great fear,
But the King had a message that you shall now hear.

King *"Prince Eric has told me what has been done.*
How the bullies were relentless and thought they had won,
But you disabled mice have been a great team,
With a presence of mind others can only dream,
And when school is finished please take up careers.
I want you to join my new Wheelchair Musketeers."

"I'm impressed you both like to eat all the right food.
Perhaps you could teach other mice what is good."
As Gerald flexed his muscles to show his physique,
The King turned to him and started to speak.
"For a mouse whose sword play is fine and elegant
It's only fitting your new name should be Quinte."

To little Ben the King now turned.
"My utter respect you have earned.
Your courage astounds me because I find
As well as lame that you are blind.
But you can serve with the Musketeers
For all of your remaining years."

Chapter 3 - Friendship And Courage

And you will take the name Appel
Reminding others you are tough as well.
A loyal colleague to be admired
A mouse of great worth and one to be hired.
Not a fool but a very clever mouse,
Who is always welcome in my house.

A mouse on whom I can depend
To deliver the mail and messages send.
I'm sure that your wheelchair will know
Which is the correct way to go."
"Your Majesty I will not fail."
And Appel bowed to end this tale.

The moral here I'm sure you'll agree
Is have respect and live happily
With all your friends and family too,
And in return they will respect you.
Being a bully is not cool
And breaks this very basic rule.

If you find someone is bullying you
Here is what you must do.
Tell someone whom you know and trust,
Like a teacher, and you must
Make sure you are not on your own
In the playground or going home.

A friend like Gerald would be ideal
Or just a companion to make you feel
Safe and secure all the time,
At home, in school and in playtime.
Stand up to bullies, don't let them win.
They should be punished for their sin.

Ben and Gerald had the right plan
To beat the bullies before they began.
If you want to grow big and strong
Healthy and wise with a life that is long.
Eat healthily and just keep fit.
Your body will appreciate it.
Do exercise to make you puff and pant,
And you too can be like Appel and Quinte.

Chapter 4 - A Big Mistake

The Wheelchair Musketeers trained hard
Outside one of the Palace's yards,
And often watching over them
The King's twin daughters, Bo and Wren.
Wren loved one particular swordsman here,
Andrew - not yet a Musketeer.

She'd sit and watch from a nearby chair,
And into his dark blue eyes would stare.
When the Wheelchair Musketeers had gone
On field manoeuvres several days long,
A group of young cadets remained
By master swordsmen to be trained.

Andrew
(Octave)

Princess Wren was in a daze,
When she had young Andrew's gaze.
She wasn't focused on what she was doing,
Her love of him would be her ruin.
The twins hadn't noticed sneaking near
Someone strangely dressed to fear.

He called them over and pretended to cry.
"I've lost me friend" he sobbed – it was a lie.
"Come with me and help me look."
The creature was a sly old crook.
But the twins were taken in.
Being kind they decided to help him.

The young cadets became aware
Something was wrong. The twins weren't there.
They were sitting here a short time ago,
But where they'd gone they didn't know.
Then they heard a piercing scream,
And saw the twins dragged to the stream.

Chapter 4 - A Big Mistake

They saw them thrown into a cart
By two rats disguised for the part.
The cadets were far too far away
To stop them or even cause delay.
The mice grabbed weapons, food and rope.
They knew they were Bo and Wren's last hope.

*"Raise the alarm for Bo and Wren.
The rats have taken them to their den."*
Three cadets took off in pursuit.
Perhaps they could memorise the route.
The alarm was raised. Appel rang the bell.
He went to tell King Mouse as well.

The bell rang loud across the fields
Alerting the Wheelchair Musketeers,
Who raced back home and to the Palace
To learn first hand about the malice.
Three cadets were in hot pursuit,
So the rest decided would follow suit.

Prime, Seconde, Quinte, Tierce and Quarte
Grabbed food and weapons and made a start.
They set off soon after the midday sun.
Another adventure had begun.
With them Balestra ran alongside
Accompanying them as their guide.

The King summoned his own Musketeers
To rescue his daughters and allay his fears.
He'd lots of faith in his wheelchair guys,
But they'd need help if the Ratland spies
Planned a counter-attack in disguise,
And sprung on them a big surprise.

Chapter 4 - A Big Mistake

So now we had an interesting race.
Three cadets first in the chase,
With the Wheelchair team two hours behind
And the King's Musketeers last in line.
But all were determined in their task
To rescue Bo and Wren and FAST.

The three cadets kept the cart in view,
As they pushed their wheelchairs gently through
The long grass and the rubble strewn
Along the pathway in pursuit.
They were sure the rats were unaware
That they were actually there.

They kept their noise down just in case
The rats should turn and spot their place.
But as the sun began to set
The three cadets crept nearer yet,
So they could work out what to do,
A plan and it's execution too.

The youngsters listened but keeping low
Were shocked to see one land a blow.
The rats had started their own fight
And argued over their own plight.
Instead of taking their captives back
They could earn big money, which they lack.

The King would pay well for his daughters,
To save them from a certain slaughter.
The three cadets were now concerned,
About this situation they learned,
And knew they needed soon to act,
Before the rats agreed their pact.

Chapter 4 - A Big Mistake

But on their own what could they do?
They were small and the rats were huge.
Then cadet Ruth had a great idea
To make them bigger, or so appear.
Create a shadow using screen and light.
Appear so big the rats would have a fright.

The mice then delved through all their gear
To see what they had that would come near
To a sheet or screen, and Jo the Mouse
Produced a really ample blouse,
Which with the rope passed through the sleeves
Would be perfect for their needs.

They made their screen and crept around
To where the rats were bedding down.
Waiting until they fell asleep
The mice would quietly nearer creep
And use the light from the camp fire
To wreak the havoc they desired.

Just then they heard a noise behind.
They lay in wait to see what they'd find.
It was the Wheelchair Musketeers
And not the enemy which they'd feared.
The three cadets relayed their plan
And what they feared for Bo and Wren.

The Musketeers thought it would be great
To add some spice and seal the fate,
Balestra should project the image
And all could then enjoy the scrimmage
When rats ran around all over the place,
Terrified of her lovely face.

Chapter 4 - A Big Mistake

So Ruth and Jo near the fire did sit
Holding the screen some way from it.
Balestra summoned her deepest roar
The rats awoke and what they saw
Projected was a large cat's head,
Assumed it was a lion and fled.

The mice knew that they, too must flee,
Back to Mouseland quick as can be.
Bo and Wren were found safe and well
And grateful that their terrifying spell
Of captivity was at an end.
Their fearfulness now on the mend.

The Princesses rode upon the back
Of Balestra the brave black and white cat.
The Musketeers sent her on her way,
To reach Mouseland by break of day,
And report to King Mouse of their deeds
And that they had no further needs.

The rest made progress through the night
And soon were joined in their flight
By the King's own Musketeers,
Who told them of King Mouse's fears,
That rats have tended to react
With a sudden counter-attack.

Chapter 4 - A Big Mistake

The Musketeers were on their guard
All the way to the Palace yard.
When they arrived the King drew his sword
And dubbed the cadets with these words,
"Though you are youngsters I give my pledge.
Over the rats you had the edge."

"You have the right maturity
To be Wheelchair Musketeers all three.
Sixte, Septime and Octave,
Please join your colleagues and work hard.
I'm so grateful you saw the twins had gone,
Rescued them and brought them home."

"Unfortunately we cannot rest,
Because I fear the rats will press
An attack upon our land again
And try to inflict a lot of pain.
I need ideas of what we can do
To prevent the rats from getting through."

The moral of this latest tale
Concerns your safety if you fail
To listen to this good advice
And learn from the mistakes of the mice,
Who left their friends and went willingly,
To help a stranger look to see,
If his lost friend could be found,
Among the flowers, I'll be bound.

But the stranger was a fraud
And not what Bo and Wren first thought.
So never go to look for sweets,
Puppies, friends or other treats.
If a stranger asks you so
Be sure to let your parents know.

If you are playing with your friends
Stay together because in the end
Just like the Wheelchair Musketeers
With safety in numbers you need not fear.

Chapter 5 - Invasion

The Wheelchair Musketeers gathered round,
To work out tactics if they found
Their wheelchairs got in the way
Of those already in the fray.
They knew they could be in the fight
While still remaining out of sight.

Sixte was a very clever mouse.
She was the one to make a blouse
And project a shadow on a screen,
To make the rats believe they'd seen
Something that filled them with great fear.
Well now she had another idea.

Her scheme was for a surprise attack
From within the walls against the back,
Of numerous rats as they ran by,
With scones and buns and even pie.
The Palace cook made rock hard cakes,
Pies, flans and other bakes.

Behind the panels on the walls,
Were secret passages known to all
The wheelchair mice their usage for
To get around from floor to floor.
By using pulleys and a clamp
Quarte made a useful lift and ramp.

Zoë (Allez)

The secret passages had two rooms,
Which could be used for treating wounds.
Providing a safe place to be
For youngsters, old and weaponry.
So Prime and Sixte went to the King
To try to sell their plan to him.

Kim (Prêt

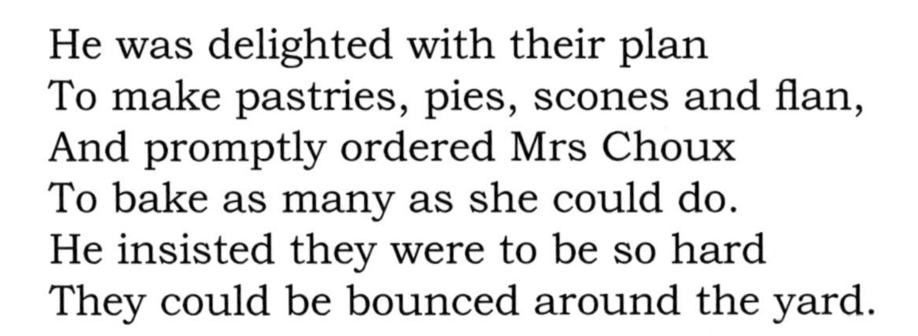

He was delighted with their plan
To make pastries, pies, scones and flan,
And promptly ordered Mrs Choux
To bake as many as she could do.
He insisted they were to be so hard
They could be bounced around the yard.

Chapter 5 - Invasion

So the Wheelchair Musketeers
Were tasked with gathering food and gear,
And storing it within the walls
To help the King when assistance calls.
They also made a treatment space,
A refuge and a hiding place.

The King sounded the Muster Call
For mice of a certain age to fall
In line at the rear Palace Gate,
And explain where they could operate.
So tiny Bill did so appear
In his brand new wheelchair.

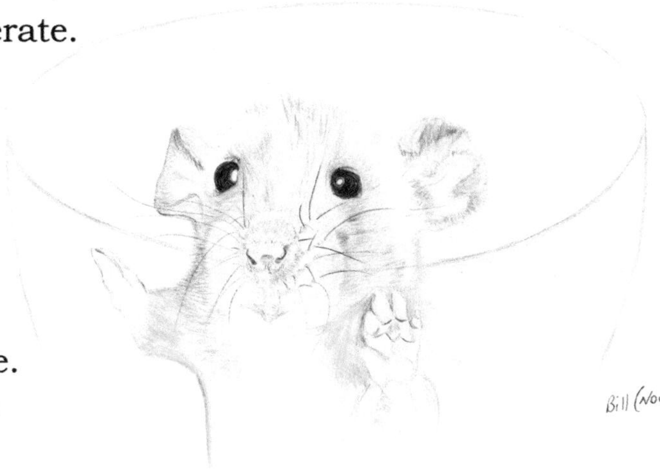

His parents had no idea he'd gone.
But loyalty where he'd come from
Was very important, so he tried
To be accepted and he lied,
About his age, said he was older.
The Sergeant had seen no one bolder.

The Commander sent him with his foil
To help the others in their toil,
To stock up with food from the cook,
Bandages, weapons, and to look,
For places ammunition would stack
To hit rats with the surprise attack.

Chapter 5 - Invasion

Tierce and Quarte while looking round,
Old catapults and sling shot found.
They distributed them far and wide,
And provided them on every side.
They also laid a small minefield
With banana skins and orange peel.

There was one more thing Quarte had to do.
Launch multiple missiles of Mrs Choux,
Simultaneously in the assault,
By modifying a catapult.
This secret weapon was so inspired
And capable of volley fire.

A number of the young and old
Were helped into the secret hold.
The Musketeers all hugged each other
And pledged to look out for their brother.
Then everyone took up position
And waited for the invasion.

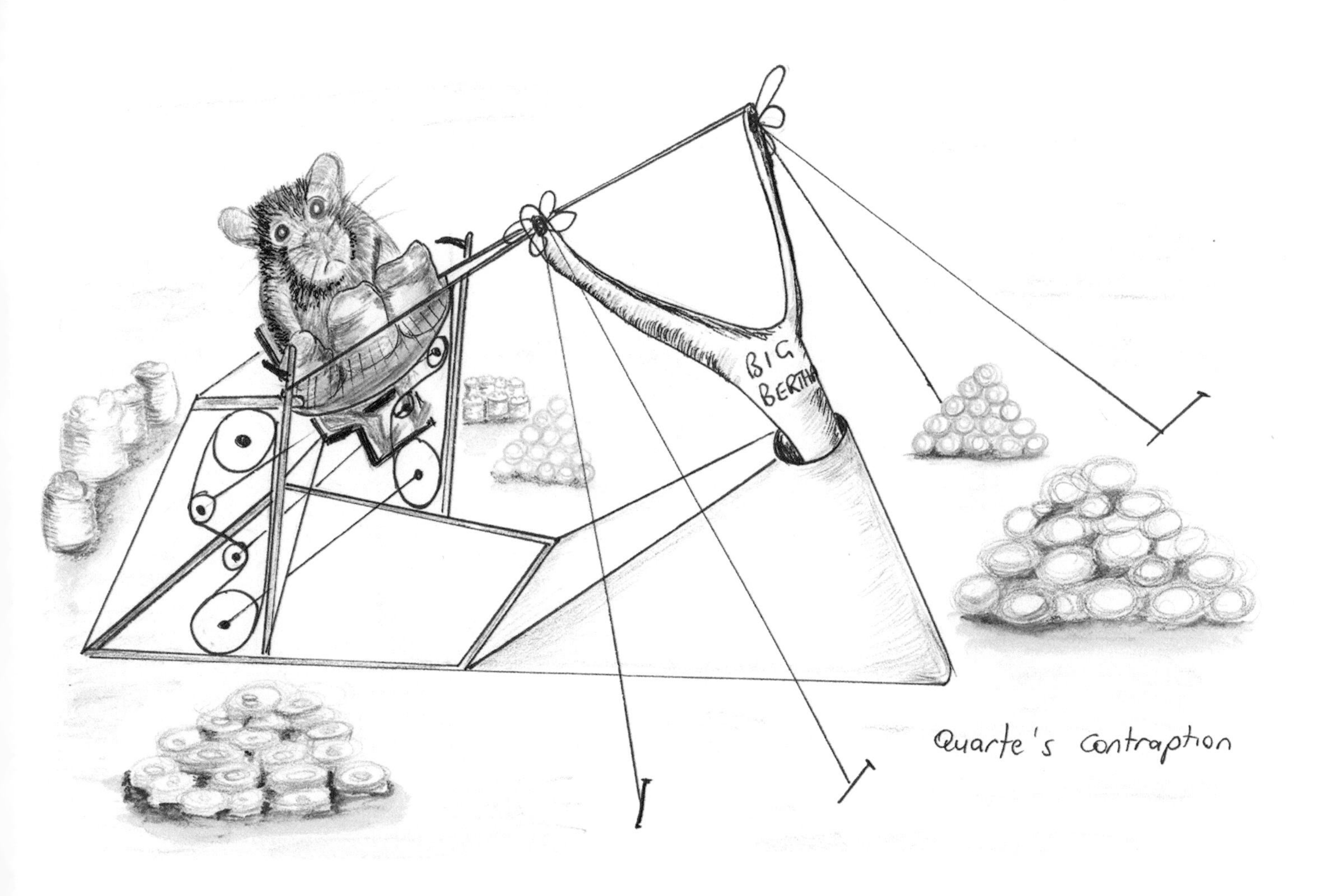

Mice occupied drawbridge and moat,
To stall intrusion by land or boat.
Soon rats appeared as large as could be,
Spread out as far as the eye could see.
The King feared for his beloved land,
Prayed he would not die at their hand.

Chapter 5 - Invasion

Beside him sat Quinte and Appel.
He sent them off to ring the bell
And relay to Prime just what they saw.
The battle now lay at their door.
The Wheelchair Musketeers were ready,
With weapons loaded, primed and steady.

So alas it wasn't long,
Before they heard a mighty throng,
Of mice and rats in battle cry,
The clash of swords all rushing by.
Tierce and Quarte kept all in view,
Via spy holes they were looking through.

When they thought the time was right
They unleashed a barrage with all their might,
Of Mrs. Choux's hardest fayre,
She'd taken hours to prepare.
Designer, Quarte, rigged up a line
And volley fired three at a time.

The rats had no idea where from.
They discontinued with their run.
Several thought a tasty scone
Was what they needed now they'd come.
Biting down on top and beneath
They broke off several of their teeth.

Chapter 5 - Invasion

Right then they saw a fearful sight.
The King, his Princes, and their plight.
With them the King's bodyguard, Flèche.
A braver mouse you'll never face,
Surrounded, and rats about to kill.
Then Prime shouted, ***"Fire at will!"***

Octave took aim and fired at once,
And scored a hit on Malone's bonce.
With sling Septime fired a sprout.
Hit a rat and knocked him out.
She reloaded with two pork pies
And hit another between the eyes.

Every cadet played their part.
Adrian launched tart after tart.
Sam used a carrot as a bat
And whacked a cup cake at a rat.
The missile missed, hit a door instead
Then bounced and hit rat on his head.

The rats seemed to advance in waves
The Musketeers running round like slaves.
Launching every cake and tart
That Mrs. Choux had baked by heart.
They even sent her back to the oven
To make and bake several more dozen.

Yet still the rats came on and on.
There were so many and very strong.
The mice wondered what could be done.
They were slowly being overrun.
Though many rats were grossly stuffed.
Out of breath and really puffed.

Kim and Zoe manned the 'gun'
'Big Bertha' the secret contraption
Built by Quarte to volley fire
Anything of their desire.
They shot out loads of vol-au-vents,
Causing absolute chaos to everyone.

Chapter 5 - Invasion

Rats couldn't see from where missiles came.
They only later felt the pain.
In the melée that ensued
Malone lunged among the food
Hoping to stab the little mouse King,
But brave Flèche took the blow for him.

Prime decided the time was right
To use the ramp and join the fight.
Max launched a barrage of covering fire.
Sam lowered the ramp to allow the retire
Of Mouse King, Princes and poor Flèche, too,
Enabling the Wheelchair Musketeers through.

The cadets stayed to hold the fort,
And prevent the others from being caught.
The rampant Wheelchair Musketeers
Drew their swords and showed no fear.
The rats thought they would catch their prey,
But the Musketeers swerved away.

Rats changed direction to follow them,
Right into a minefield whereupon
They skidded, slipped and slid about,
And fell on bottom, head and snout.
But still the rats came on and on.
There was just no getting rid of them.

Eventually the Musketeers
Had clean run out of fresh ideas.
Exhausted they were overrun,
With nowhere left for them to turn.
But tiny Bill who'd joined the team,
Saw something as a very last scheme.

Chapter 5 - Invasion

He needed to get across the hall,
To a specific point right by the wall.
Away from his fellow Musketeers,
Whom he must deter from coming near.
The Musketeers continued to fence
A rearguard action in defence.

Bill drew his sword and charged as well.
He stabbed and lunged in a frenzied spell.
His act was stopped when grabbed by a rat,
Thrown down on the floor with a splat.
The rat then tried to sit on him
But a well-aimed pie made him spin.

Unfortunately Bill was so small,
He couldn't reach their bodies at all,
And so he stabbed them in the knee
Or whatever body parts he could see.
The rat grabbed him a second time.
And tied his hands up with a line.

Bill was face down on the floor,
The rat astride him as before.
He struggled to free his fencing hand,
To finish the mission as he planned.
It was such an effort just to breathe,
Just then Balestra charged at speed.

She barged into the big fat rat,
Dislodged him from his cosy chat.
Enough to loosen the piece of cord,
Enabling Bill to grab his sword,
And with the speed of a rocket
He plunged it into an electric socket.

A bang, a flash, explosion too,
Fire, sparks and smoke black and blue.
The rats were blown right off their feet
And landed in a massive heap.
The sprinkler system now turned on
With water pouring from every one.

The valiant mice returned via the ramp
To the safety of their camp.
They gently carried tiny Bill
And placed him near the window sill.
They watched the panic of their foe
As they splashed about down below.

Chapter 5 - Invasion

Water gushed through every room.
Along corridors and very soon
It gushed down walls and down the stairs.
It washed away tables and chairs.
The torrent washed rats down the drain
Never to be seen again.

When the dust had settled down
Everyone gathered round.
As tiny Bill was lying there,
Badly burned and unaware.
No one knew if he would live or die.
The other mice began to cry.

Chapter 5 - Invasion

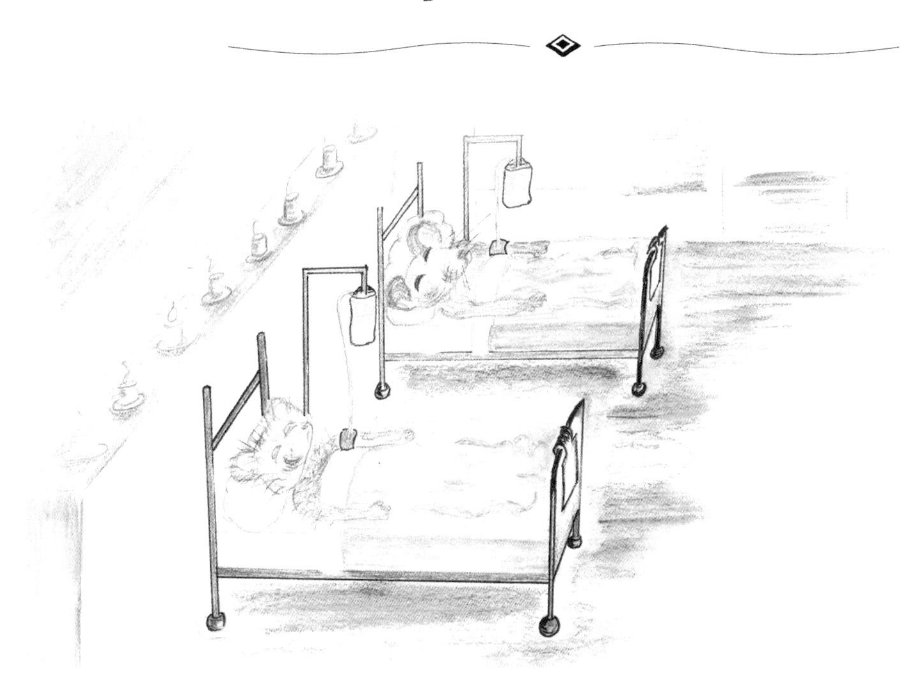

Bill and Flèche were carried by all
To the makeshift hospital in the wall,
Where they both lay so very still.
As their colleagues kept an all-night vigil.
Bill, when he awoke was sore.
His fur all gone and his skin raw.

Flèche also managed to recover.
His wounds severe as he soon discovered
While he was lying on a board.
The knife had severed his spinal cord.
So he would never walk again,
Just like his many wheelchair friends.

The King was very much dismayed
A mix of emotions he displayed.
Horror at what happened to his land.
Grateful for loyal folk at hand.
Visited the sick to say *"Thank you"*
To tiny Bill and dear Flèche too.

To Bill he said, *"You are so small,*
But you are the bravest mouse of all,
Because you answered the Muster Call
And fought so valiantly through it all.
So we now honour this tiny gem.
From now on you are Nouvième."

To Flèche he said, *"And now dear friend*
I'm determined this won't be the end
You've served me long and faithfully
I must now reward such loyalty.
So you will have a new career
And lead the Wheelchair Musketeers."

Chapter 5 - Invasion

The moral of this final tail
Take care of youngsters and the frail.
Be strong in the face of adversity,
Caring, honest and you will see
With friendship, truth and loyalty
You'll build a fair society.

A word of advice to all concerned,
There's one more thing you should have learned.
To avoid being lit up like a rocket
NEVER, EVER poke something into an electric socket.

The King now turned to those behind
Saying, *"I have something on my mind.*
You young cadets were brave throughout,
And I'd be missing something out
If not to treat you all the same
And give you each a fencing name.
So Forté, Touche and Martingale
Be loyal, determined and you won't fail."

"Young Kim and Zoe, what can I say.
Your vol-au-vent epic caused dismay
And frightened many rats away.
You new names shall be Prêt and Allez."

The King was pleased his task complete.
A troupe of Musketeers at his feet.
All eager for their sword to lend
For King and Country to defend.

The Cast

Wheelchair Musketeers	Prime	Mouse
	Seconde	Hugh
	Tierce	Jon
	Quarte	Lee
	Quinte	Gerald
	Sixte	Ruth
	Septime	Jo
	Octave	Andrew
	Nouvième	Bill
Cadets	Martingale	Adrian
	Touche	Sam
	Forté	Max
	Prêt	Kim
	Allez	Zoe
Staff	Appel	Ben
	Balestra	Cat
	Wheelchair Musketeer Captain	Flèche
Mouse Royalty	King Claud	
	Queen Phyllis	
	Prince Rupert	
	Prince Crispin	
	Prince Eric	
	Princess Bo	
	Princess Wren	
Rat Royalty	King Rat Malone	

The Epilogue

And so the story is finally done.
The rats were beaten. The mice had won.
Like them you too can learn to fence.
And have great fun at little expense.
At www.britishfencing.com
Just find a club and come along.

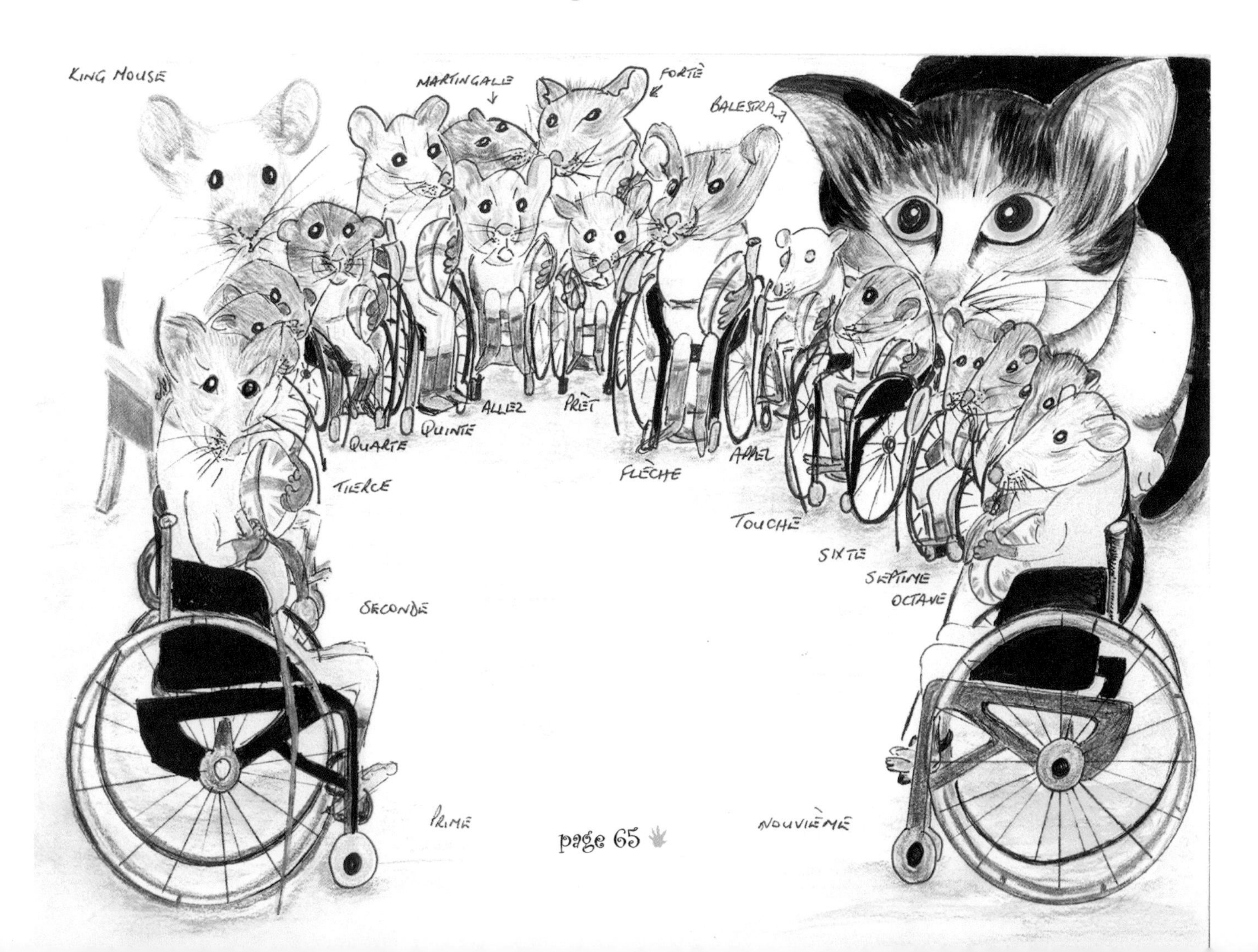

Potted History of Fencing

The sport of fencing has its origins as far back as Roman times, but the weapons were refined during the Medieval period and in 1500 the first fencing manual was produced. In the 18th Century the types of weapons changed. The rapier was replaced by the fleuret or foil as the training weapon and in the late 18th Century right-of-way conventions were introduced to make the sport much safer. In the 1850's the épée became the main duelling weapon of choice in Europe, and the sabre was adopted as the national weapon of Hungary.

In 1913 the Fédération Internationale d'Escrime (FIE) was founded. It is still the organisation that determines the rules and regulations of the sport. All the current terminology of the sport is based on the old French language.

Glossary of Fencing Terms

Pronunciation is shown in brackets

Escrime (es creem) – The French term for Fencing
Foil, Épée, Sabre – the three fencing weapons in the modern sport

En Garde (on guard) – the 'get ready' position.
Prêt (pret) – 'are you ready'
Allez (allay) – GO

The nine garde positions.

Prime (preem) – protects the chest and lower target on the non-sword arm side
Seconde (se cond) – protects the flank and lower target on the sword arm side
Tierce (tears) – protects from lateral cuts to the flank and head
Quarte (cart) – protects the head and chest against lateral cuts
Quinte (cant) – protects the head against vertical cuts
Sixte (seest) – a high line guard on the sword arm side
Septime (sep teem) – a low line guard on the non-sword arm side
Octave (oc tarve) – a low line guard on the sword arm side
Nouvième (noo-vee-em) – a high guard to protect against attacks at high level, such as a flick, or attacks round the back. It is seldom mentioned in fencing today.

Attack

Appel – beating the piste with the ball of the foot often followed by balestra
Balestra – a short sharp jump forwards, often used as a preparation for attack
Cut-through – an attacking move with the sabre, cutting the opponent in a diagonal movement across the torso.
Flèche (flaysh) the French word for arrow) – an alternative way of reaching your opponent at foil and épée, where both feet leave the ground and for a second the body is near horizontal
Lunge – an attacking move where the fencer rapidly closes the distance towards an opponent and simultaneously extends the arm and sword to hit the target.

Defence

Parry – the action of defending
Riposte – and hitting back.

Foible – the weakest part of the blade near the tip
Forté (fortay)- the strongest part of the blade near the hand guard
Martingale – a leather loop fitted between the guard pad and the handle of a French-handle foil, held to prevent the weapon being pulled out of the fencer's hand. (1)
Touche (toosh) – an indication of a hit on target

Know the Game Fencing, 2nd Edition. Author – British Fencing.
Published by A&C Black Publishers Ltd, 38, Soho Square, London W1D 3HB in 2007

Special Thanks

My thanks go to all the wheelchair fencers and staff past and present who provided such a rich tapestry from which to work.

Mat Campbell-Hill, Natalie Child, Jonathan Collins, Gemma Collis-McCann, Dimitri Coutya, Piers Gilliver, Tom Hall-Butcher, Emily Holder, Justine Moore, Duncan Moyes, Kasjan Paszkowski, Dan Puckey, Rebecca Puckey, Shah Rashid, Alan Sheriff, Dan Smith, James Thomas, Josh Waddell and Justine Willmott.

I would also like to thank Fiona and Alan Sheriff for helping with proof reading and advice on the suitability of the written material.

Special thanks go to Helen Kewell and her happy little brood for road-testing the words and pictures, twice!

Finally I owe a great deal to my brother, Simon and sister-in-law, Biddy who were critical with their feedback on the illustrations, and also for putting the finished article together.

The picture of two mice on page 32 is a drawing from a photograph of 'George and Mildred the mice in a log pile house' reproduced by kind permission of Simon Dell of Simon Dell Photography.

Other pictures in this book, on pages 12, 13, 32, 38 and 39 are drawings reproduced from photographs in "Collins Complete Guide to British Animals" first published by Harper Collins Publishers Limited in 2005, and reissued in 2010.

Printed in Poland
by Amazon Fulfillment
Poland Sp. z o.o., Wrocław

51219948R00042